Stories and rhymes in this book

A catalogue record for this book is available from the British Library

Published by Ladybird Books Ltd
27 Wrights Lane London W8 5TZ
A Penguin Company
© LADYBIRD BOOKS LTD MCMXCIX
Produced for Ladybird Books Ltd by Nicola Baxter and Amanda Hawkes
The moral rights of the author/illustrator have been asserted
LADYBIRD and the device of a Ladybird are trademarks of Ladybird Books Ltd

The Mystery Mice

by Ronne Randall

illustrated by Marjolein Pottie

Ladybird

CALL THE MICE!

To solve any mystery,
Don't think twice,

You just have to call
On the Mystery Mice.

Minerva will gaze in her crystal ball.

Magnus' methods will show him all!

But if you want to know the FACTS...

Call the littlest of all, who's known as Max.

THE MYSTERY PRESENT

Aunt Millicent had sent the Mystery Mice a present.

"It's a beautiful silver tray," said Minerva, unwrapping the parcel.

"I see swirling patterns, like waves in the sea. WW must stand for Wild Waves.

Perhaps Aunt Millicent is telling us that there will be a storm at sea!"

Max wasn't sure his dad was right.

"I will solve the mystery by gazing into my crystal ball," said Minerva.

"I see...
swirling,
snowy mists.
WW must
stand for
White Winter.

Aunt
Millicent
is telling us
that we will
have snow
this winter!"

Max still wasn't certain.
He turned the tray round.
"That's it!" he exclaimed.

"It doesn't say WW at all.
It says MM. And MM
stands for... Mystery Mice!"

ALL ABOUT MICE

Mice have twitchety whiskers,

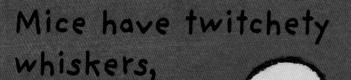

And mice have fidgety tails,

And mice have sniffety noses,

That follow
mysterious trails!

THE MYSTERIOUS NEIGHBOUR

"I have a new neighbour," Agatha Rabbit told her friend Minerva.

"But I haven't seen hair nor tail of him... or her.

Yet every
night I hear
strange
scuffling
sounds
coming from
the garden.

It's a real
mystery,
Minerva."

"Mysteries are made to be solved!" cried Minerva.

"I see water..." said Minerva, gazing into her ball, "maybe even a ship.

Your new neighbour must be a pirate!

He's burying stolen treasure in his garden!"

"I hope he hasn't got a cutlass!" said Agatha.

All at once Eloise Rabbit and Max Mystery Mouse rushed in from Agatha's garden.

"Come and see what we've discovered!" they said.

"Look," said Max, peering through the bushes.

"So THAT'S my new neighbour!" said Agatha.

"It's Diggery Mole!"

Diggery, catching sight of them, invited everyone into his garden.

"Last night I finished digging out my new swimming pool," he said.

"As soon as it's filled, I'm having a swimming party for my friends and neighbours.

I hope you'll all come."

And of course,
they all did!

MANY MYSTERIES

There are scary mysteries,

And hairy mysteries,

And mysteries that wriggle.

But the mysteries
I like best of all...

Are the ones that make you giggle!

MYSTERIOUS MESSAGES

One morning, Max woke up
and saw footprints
on the floor
of his room.

He followed
them all the
way to...

his bookshelf and found
a note:

The trail ends here.
Now you must go
To the cupboard
down below!

"That must
mean the
cupboard
under the
stairs," said
Max. So he
hurried
downstairs.

In the cupboard, Max
found another note.

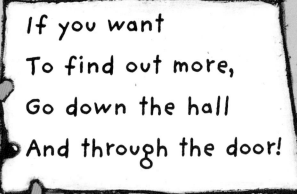

If you want
To find out more,
Go down the hall
And through the door!

"How very
mysterious!"
said Max.
He went
through
the kitchen
door to
find a...

"SURPRISE!"

cried Mum, Dad, Aunt
Millicent, Agatha Rabbit,
Eloise and Diggery Mole.
"HAPPY BIRTHDAY, MAX!"

Max was SO happy. He opened his present from Mum and Dad first.

"Thank you!" he cried. "My very own magnifying glass!"

"You're welcome, son," said
Magnus and Minerva.
"Now you're a REAL
Mystery Mouse!"

A MISTY MYSTERY

Gazing in my crystal ball,
I see someone very tall.

Or is it someone very small?
I'm not really sure at all!

THE MYSTERIOUS MINT THIEF

Magnus Mouse settled down in his favourite armchair.

"Time for a Mystic Mint," he said.

Max and Magnus looked carefully for clues.

"Dad! Look!" said Max.

There was a Mystic Mint on the hall floor.

"Look!" said Max. "There are mints on the stairs!"

The Mystic Mint trail led right to a big wardrobe.

"The thief must be hiding in there," whispered Magnus.

"Stand back, son!"

S-l-o-w-l-y
Magnus
opened
the door.

But inside there were only
some clothes...

and the
empty hanger
for Magnus'
cardigan.

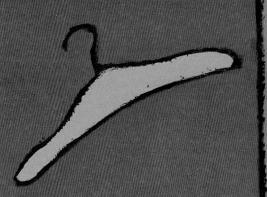

All at once,
Max had
an idea.

"Dad," he said, "are you SURE there's nothing in your pocket?"

Magnus checked. "Nothing at all," he said, looking sheepishly at his son, "except... a hole!"

THE MYSTERIOUS MOUSE

A very mysterious mouse
Is creeping about the house.

On the
stairs,

Behind
chairs,

Who IS that mysterious mouse?

Hunt in crannies and cracks, And you might just find...

MAX!